T0132197

RISING KINGDOM

ELANA KOBB

Rising Kingdom

iUniverse books may be ordered through booksellers or by contacting:

iUniverse
1663 Liberty Drive
Bloomington, IN 47403
www.iuniverse.com
1-800-Authors (1-800-288-4677)

Credits for the author picture:
Leisl Steinbach
Leisl Elisabeth Photography

ISBN: 978-1-5320-8300-6 (sc)
ISBN: 978-1-5320-8301-3 (e)

Library of Congress Control Number: 2019913791

Print information available on the last page.

iUniverse rev. date: 09/11/2019

RISING KINGDOM

Another day in the jungle, another night somewhere else,

The morning's normal chirping, the sound of many bells.

The grass warm and green, the water simply glimmering

While clouds still with the sun, caused a great shimmering.

Everyone knew where they stood in class,

But very soon that changed, very, very fast.

Every week animals gave their king a portion of food,

Lions received these taxes and the matter brightened their mood.

But not the others, they loathed this event that was every week.

For reform and some changes, they would always seek.

After many years of complete contentment,

A subtle longing arose, of pure lion resentment.

The toucans cried "Why must we listen to one who doesn't know,

What goes on above land, or down below?"

As the night grew cold and dark, the stars twinkled with hope.

It seemed as if they all were standing on tightropes.

The water was violent, the sky filled with commotion,

The clouds whisked and stirred the vast ocean.

The whales cried "Why must we listen to one who doesn't know,

What goes on above land, or down below?"

Lions controlled the kingdom and everything found in it.

The bright colorful land, soon became dull and grey-tinted.

Dissatisfaction arose and friends turned to foes,

A hummingbird cried "Why must we listen to one who doesn't know,

What goes on above land, or down below?"

It was a sunny day in the jungle lands,

The lions held the world in the palms of their hands.

The sharks and birds, their anger grew,

They spread the word, and demanded something new.

The monkeys wrote down their thoughts on the jungle trees

"Why do we listen to these feline fiends?

We must reject their unkindly rule,

We must all get together and challenge them to a duel!

If we gain enough support, the cause will surely succeed.

No longer will we have to give up our weekly pay in feed."

So when many were educated and all became aware,

Sky and sea joined forces, and hastily prepared.

As a symbol of rebel and revolt that went against

The lions and their followers, at their expense.

Sky and sea gathered their stored up food

Just to prove a point, although it was crude.

They made a great fire, as large as could be,

An attempt to burn the food, and set themselves free.

Many gathered together from the sky and sea in fact,

Fought the lions and cats, again and again they attacked.

It was a gruesome battle, the lions won...almost.

The battle was a scary one, the sides were so close.

But the sea and sky were victorious, they won without one lost.

And now that sky and sea won, the lions paid a cost.

The sky and sea proposed, with absolute control

"The lions must contribute a twice weekly toll.

If they are against the revolution, they will soon see,

To Antarctica they'll be sent, yes, they will be!"

The lions quickly were hungry, just as the others were,

And the same thing that happened, once again occurred.

A bird was crowned Queen, and a whale was crowned King.

The whale raised its tail and the bird raised its wing.

The rule went to separate lands, separate lands indeed.

No more paying lions taxes of weekly pay in feed.

And the days grew happier and everyone well fed,

That is the finishing of our story, this is...THE END

Printed in the United States
By Bookmasters